Sticker swaps

written by Marie Birkinshaw
illustrated by Peter Stevenson

Here are
some boys.

Here are some
football fans.

Here are some
football players.

Here are
some shops.

Here are some
football books.

Here are some
football stickers.

Swap you!

Just right!

written by Lorraine Horsley
illustrated by Amanda Wood

Too big,

too small,

just right for me.

Too big,

too small,

just right for me.

Too big,

too small,

just right for me.

Too big, too small.

This is just right
for me!

Good day, bad day!

written by Lorraine Horsley
illustrated by Toni Goffe

Good boy,

bad boy!

Good girl,

bad girl!

Good baby,

bad baby!

Good cat,

bad cat!

Good dog,

bad dog!

Good day,

bad day.

Good night!

Purr-fect puss

written by Lorraine Horsley
illustrated by Paula Martyr

I'm happy.

I'm sad.

I'm good.

I'm bad.

I'm cold.

I'm hot.

I'm hungry.

Now I'm not.

New words introduced in this book

cat   good   bad

cold   hot

happy   sad   hungry

are, for, here, just, not, now,

Messy mud!

Ben and his puppy are in the mud, in a mess, in trouble! Read the story to your child and talk about the pictures together. This story uses the names of the rooms in a house.

Rollercoaster ride

This rhyme introduces new words to your child in a lively and humorous way. How are some of the rollercoaster riders feeling at the end of their ride? Would your child be feeling sick after all that twisting and turning – or would she enjoy it?

New words

These are the words that help to tell the stories and rhymes in this book. Try looking through the book together to find some of the words again.

(Vocabulary used in the titles of the stories is not listed.)

is specially designed to help your child learn to read. It will complement all the methods used in schools.

Parents took part in extensive research to ensure that **Read with Ladybird** would help your child to:

- take the first steps in reading
- improve early reading progress
- gain confidence in new-found abilities.

The research highlighted that the most important qualities in helping children to read were that:

- books should be fun – children have enough 'hard work' at school
- books should be colourful and exciting
- stories should be up to date and about everyday experiences
- repetition and rhyme are especially important in boosting a child's reading ability.

The stories and rhymes introduce the 100 words most frequently used in reading and writing.

These 100 key words actually make up half the words we use in speech and reading.

The three levels of **Read with Ladybird** consist of 22 books, taking your child from two words per page to 600-word stories.

Read with Ladybird will help your child to master the basic reading skills so vital in everyday life.

Ladybird have successfully published reading schemes and programmes for the last 50 years. Using this experience and the latest research, **Read with Ladybird** has been produced to give all children the head start they deserve.

Purr-fect puss

Enjoy reading this rhyme to your child. He may
remember that he has met the words 'good' and 'bad'
in *Good day, bad day!* The rhyme will help your child to
guess – and then to remember – what the words are.
It also introduces the contraction *I'm* instead of *I am*.

New words

These are the words that help to tell the stories and
rhymes in this book. Try looking at the
book again to find some of the words.
(Vocabulary used in the
titles of the stories
is not listed.)

Read with Ladybird...

is specially designed to help your child learn to read. It will complement all the methods used in schools.

Parents took part in extensive research to ensure that **Read with Ladybird** would help your child to:

- take the first steps in reading
- improve early reading progress
- gain confidence in new-found abilities.

The research highlighted that the most important qualities in helping children to read were that:

- books should be fun – children have enough 'hard work' at school
- books should be colourful and exciting
- stories should be up to date and about everyday experiences
- repetition and rhyme are especially important in boosting a child's reading ability.

The stories and rhymes introduce the 100 words most frequently used in reading and writing.

These 100 key words actually make up half the words we use in speech and reading.

The three levels of **Read with Ladybird** consist of 22 books, taking your child from two words per page to 600-word stories.

Read with Ladybird will help your child to master the basic reading skills so vital in everyday life.

Ladybird have successfully published reading schemes and programmes for the last 50 years. Using this experience and the latest research, **Read with Ladybird** has been produced to give all children the head start they deserve.